Published in 2023
by Vision Australia
454 Glenferrie Road,
Kooyong, Victoria 3144

Produced by
Berbay Publishing
PO Box 133
Kew East
Victoria 3102

Vision Australia gratefully acknowledges
the generous support from The Elliot Family Trust

Printed in China

National Library of Australia
Cataloguing-in-publication data:
Dickson, John
Nikki Hind: Dressed for Success

For primary school children
ISBN 978-0-6455584-2-5

NIKKI HIND

DRESSED FOR SUCCESS

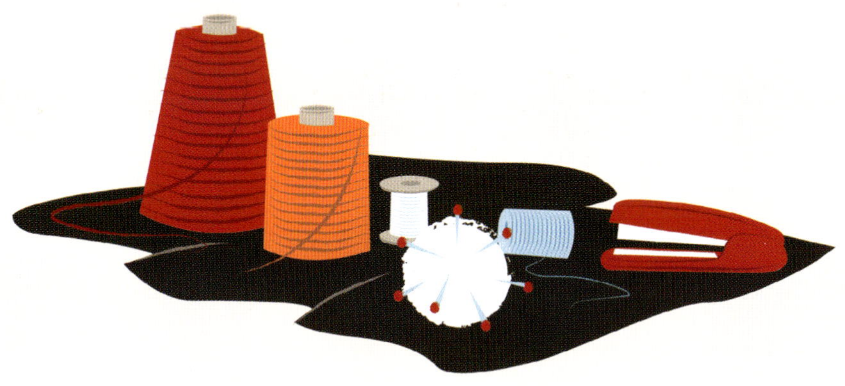

Written by John Dickson
Illustrated by Chantel de Sousa

Nikki Hind is a fashion designer. She uses her imagination to dream up beautiful clothing. But when her designs are made into clothes, she can't see them very well. Because Nikki is almost completely blind.

When Nikki was little, nobody knew that she had trouble seeing. When she was six, a doctor visited her primary school to test all the children's eyesight. Nikki was asked to read some big letters with her left eye. But she couldn't read any of them. So, she was given a patch for her eye and glasses so thick they looked like they were made from the bottoms of soft drink bottles.

Nikki was very shy at school. She struggled with learning to read, which made her very tired. She also had trouble playing sports. She could not see speeding balls or work out how far away things were. However, Nikki was really good at swimming and diving. She was best at backstroke and won awards for her diving.

Even though she was shy, Nikki's clothes made her stand out. Her friends called her 'Barbie' because she was tall and blonde, and everyone liked the way she dressed. Nikki didn't have a sewing machine, so she would hand sew clothes. When she became tired using a needle and thread, she would use a stapler!

When she was eleven, Nikki joined the circus. She lived with her mum on a small farm with lots of animals, and she trained them all to do tricks. A visitor from the Flying Fruit Fly Circus saw Nikki put on a show with her dog, Sheba, and asked them to be part of the circus. Sheba would jump through Nikki's arms, run an obstacle course, climb ladders and dance on her hind legs.

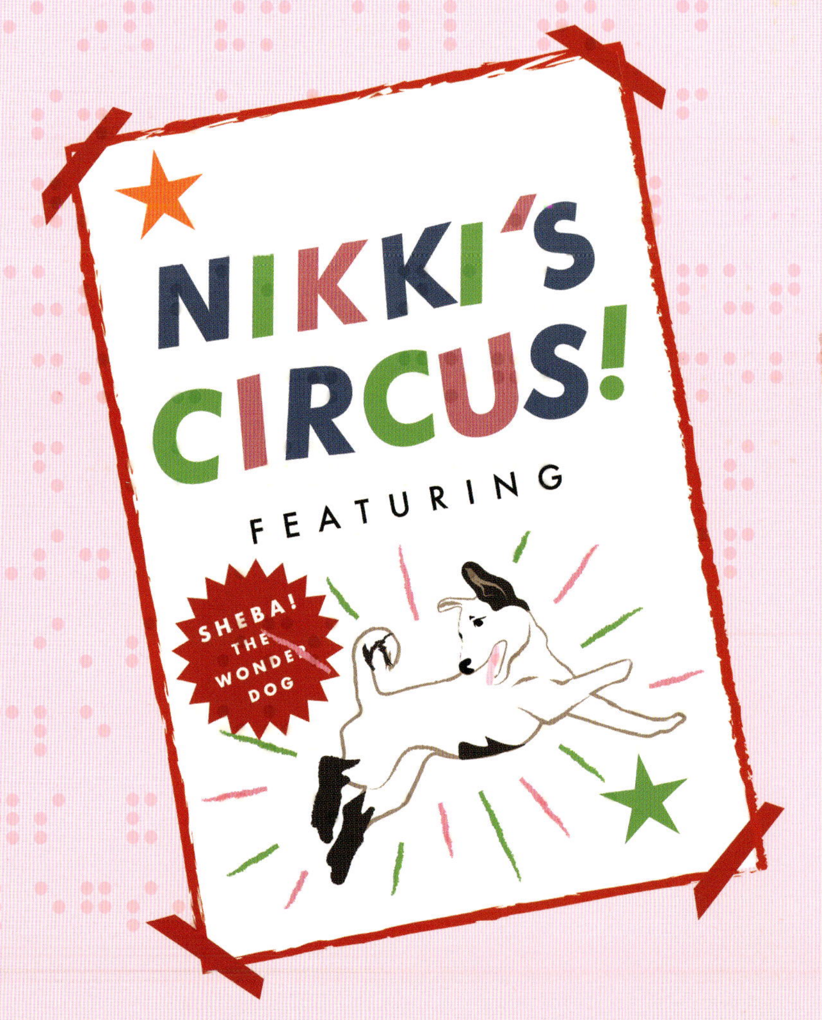

When the audience applauded, Sheba would run around and let everyone give her a pat.

NIKKI'S CIRCUS!

Nikki loved to dress up. She learned that different clothes made her feel confident in different ways. She could be a film star, a princess, or a pop star performing in front of a million people. Nikki wanted to become a fashion designer and make other people feel confident, too.

Nikki dreamed of being a model for the awards show. And one day she was. She wore a special red dress and was seen on television all over Australia. She dreamed that soon people all around the world would see the clothes she had imagined making.

Just before she became a mum, Nikki had a stroke that stole almost all of the rest of her eyesight. From then on, she could only see out of half of her right eye. Nikki didn't have time to worry much about being blind, though. She was too busy looking after her two little boys.

When her sons went to school, Nikki started thinking about going back to work. People told her that she would never work again. But she didn't believe them. She knew that all the things she had learned from being blind had made her very strong.

MEL URNE
FAS WEEK

It was time to become the fashion designer she had always wanted to be. Nikki went back to school to learn more about how to make clothes properly—without a stapler!

So, Nikki decided to create her own fashion label. She invited people with other disabilities to help her. She knew disabled people were very strong in many ways and wanted everybody to know that, too. To celebrate the hard work it took to succeed when others said she couldn't, Nikki decided to call her fashion label 'Blind Grit'.

BLIND
GRIT

Most of the people who work with Nikki at Blind Grit have a disability or have had an accident that changed their lives. None of them have let this stop them from doing amazing things. They are models, photographers, graphic designers, hairdressers, makeup artists and web designers. They all work together to show Nikki's fashion designs to the world.

Now, Nikki and her team show Blind Grit clothes as part of Melbourne Fashion Week, the most important fashion event in Australia. And people all over the world see Nikki's designs.

Nikki says, 'Don't let anything get in the way of what you are good at. When you are told that you can't do something you know that you can do easily and well, just keep going!'

GLOSSARY

Flying Fruit Fly Circus
An Australian circus for young people aged between 8 and 19 years. Students learn circus training and attend regular classes.

Grit
The ability to keep working to achieve your dreams and goals even when it's difficult.

Stroke
A stroke is when a blockage or other problem stops blood going to part of the brain. When that happens, part of the brain stops working well and it can't send signals to the body to work properly.

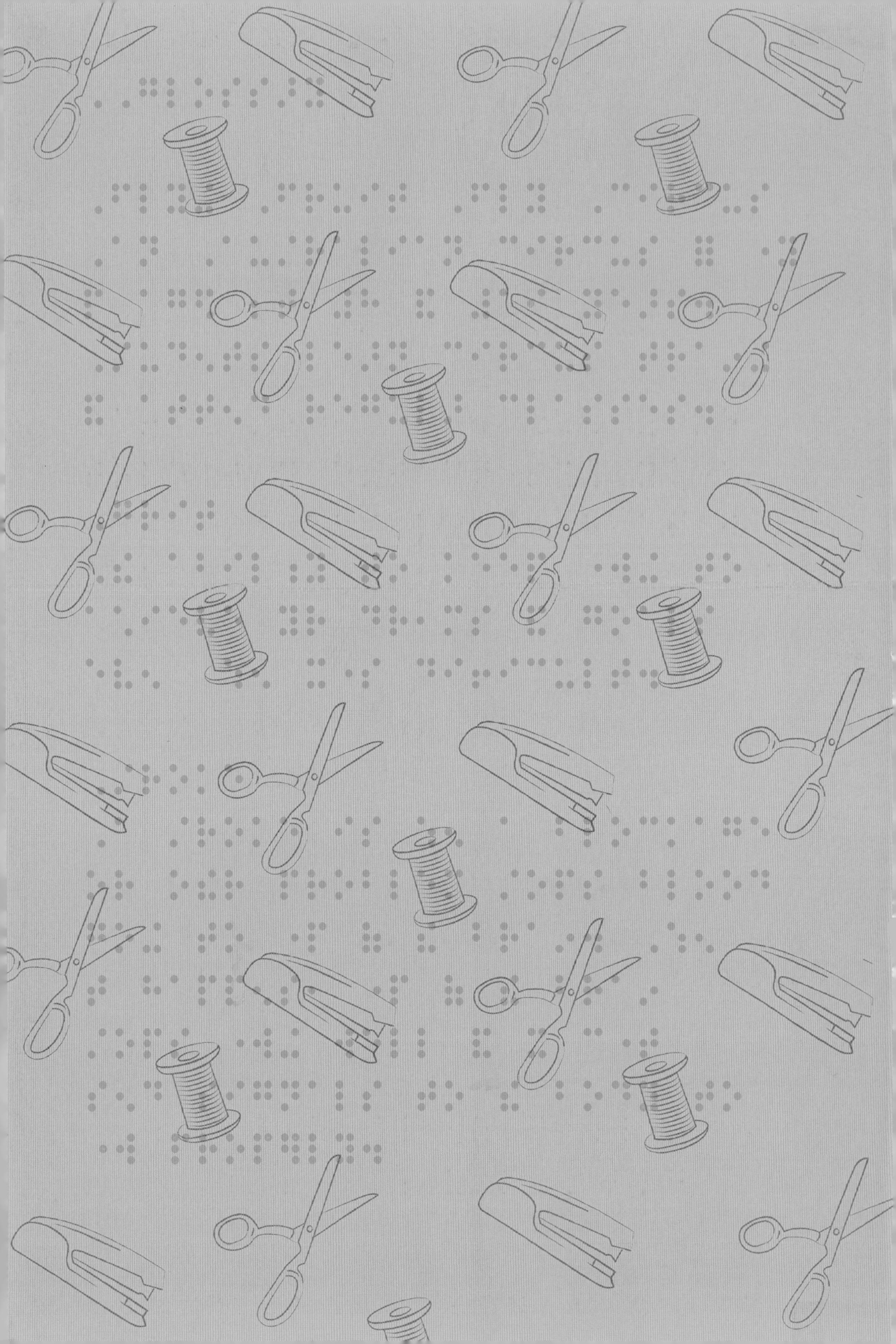